Creeksi
13563
Moreno
D0399330
E
ARN
16511

Dear Parent:

Buckle up! You are about to join your child on a very exciting journey. The destination? Independent reading!

Road to Reading will help you and your child get there. The program offers books at five levels, or Miles, that accompany children from their first attempts at reading to successfully reading on their own. Each Mile is paved with engaging stories and delightful artwork.

Getting Started
For children who know the alphabet and are eager to begin reading
• easy words • fun rhythms • big type • picture clues

Reading With Help
For children who recognize some words and sound out others with help
• short sentences • pattern stories • simple plotlines

Reading On Your Own
For children who are ready to read easy stories by themselves
• longer sentences • more complex plotlines • easy dialogue

First Chapter Books
For children who want to take the plunge into chapter books
• bite-size chapters • short paragraphs • full-color art

Chapter Books
For children who are comfortable reading independently
• longer chapters • occasional black-and-white illustrations

There's no need to hurry through the Miles. Road to Reading is designed without age or grade levels. Children can progress at their own speed, developing confidence and pride in their reading ability no matter what their age or grade.

So sit back and enjoy the ride—every Mile of the way!

Dedicated to Ali and the family of skunks
who live down the hill
M.D.A.

Library of Congress Cataloging-in-Publication Data
Arnold, Marsha Diane.
The Tail of Little Skunk / by Marsha Diane Arnold ; illustrated by Michael Terry.
p. cm. — (Road to reading. Mile 2)
Summary: Little Skunk worries about how he will escape if Big Bear comes down from the mountain.
ISBN 0-307-26218-9 (pbk.) — ISBN 0-307-46218-8 (GB)
[1. Skunks—Fiction. 2. Bears—Fiction.] I. Terry, Michael, ill. II. Title. III. Series.

PZ7.A7363 Tr 2002
[E]—dc21

2001040497

A GOLDEN BOOK • New York

ISBN: 0-307-26218-9 (pbk)
ISBN: 0-307-46218-8 (GB)

Printed in the United States of America June 2002

10 9 8 7 6 5 4 3 2

The Tail of Little Skunk

by Marsha Diane Arnold
illustrated by Michael Terry

Little Skunk
lived in a forest at the
bottom of a mountain.

On top of the mountain
lived Big Bear.

Little Skunk had never
seen Big Bear.
But every morning
he heard his roar.

Big Bear's roar made
Little Skunk shiver all over.

“What will you do
if Big Bear comes?”
Little Skunk asked Deer.
“I will run faster
than the wind,” said Deer.
“Big Bear will not catch me.”

Little Skunk felt
the wind rush past.

"I cannot run faster
than the wind," he said.

“What will you do
if Big Bear comes?”
Little Skunk asked Blue Jay.
“I will fly into the sky,”
said Blue Jay.
“Big Bear will not follow me.”

Little Skunk looked up
at the wide, blue sky.

"I cannot fly
into the sky," he said.

"What will you do
if Big Bear comes?"
Little Skunk asked Fish.
"I will swim to the
middle of the lake," said Fish.
"Big Bear will not swim
that far."

Little Skunk listened
to the sound of
the deep, blue water.

"I cannot swim to the middle of the lake," he said.

Little Skunk sat by
the edge of the lake.
He shivered for a long time.
"I cannot run fast, fly high,
or swim far,"
Little Skunk told his mother.

"What will I do
if Big Bear comes?"
asked Little Skunk.

"You are a skunk,"
said his mother.

“Skunks don’t run fast.
Skunks don’t fly high.
Skunks don’t swim far.
But you will know
what to do if Big Bear comes.
I promise!”

One morning Little Skunk
heard Big Bear's roar.
The roar sounded very loud.

Big Bear was right behind him!

“What will I do?
What will I do?
Big Bear has come!”
Little Skunk cried.

Big Bear raised his paws high.
Little Skunk raised
his tail high.
Pffft!

Big Bear roared and roared . . .
. . . and ran all the way back
to the top of the mountain.

"I am a skunk,"
Little Skunk said proudly.
"And I knew just what to do
when Big Bear came."